Tales of Friendship Grove

# In Grandpaw's Pawprints

## A Story of Loss, Life, & Love

written by Lauren Mosback          illustrated by Nino Aptsiauri

For my parents, Chris and Gayl (Pop-Pop and Gigi):

Thank you for shining your love and light all around.

We all strive to follow in your footsteps.

Love you now and forever.

In Grandpaw's
Pawprints

In Grandpaw's Pawprints

Published by Empowering Kids Media

ISBN 978-1-7350030-5-4 (Paperback)
ISBN 978-1-7350030-6-1 (Hardcover)

LAURENMOSBACK.COM

Meet Our Friends!

# Ona the Eagle
Leader of Friendship Grove. Protective;
Caring; Empowering.

# Riley the Racoon
Charismatic; Empathetic.
Loves to problem-solve.

# Martin the Mountain Lion
Kind; Wise; Artistic. Loves to bake and paint.

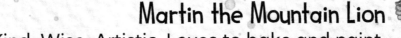

# Faye the Fox
Quick-witted; Playful; Loyal.
Loves sports and games.

# Bethany the Bear
Brave; Generous; Musical.
Loves to play the guitar and sing.

# Grandpaw
Bethany's Grandfather

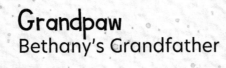

Riley the Raccoon climbed out of bed and tiptoed to his window. As he looked outside, he saw a blanket of snow covering Friendship Grove, inviting him to play.

After eating a bowl of blackberry oatmeal, Riley raced to meet his friends, Martin the Mountain Lion and Faye the Fox.

Faye made circles in the snow, and Martin caught a wet snowflake on his tongue. Riley's heart thumped with excitement. He wanted Bethany the Bear to play, too—but the colder it became, the more she slept. Familiar laughter woke her today, though, so she joined her friends in the snow.

Together, the Woodland Crew played hide-and-seek and went sledding on Harmony Hill. They made snow angels and admired their unique shapes in the snow. "Let's build a snow animal!" Bethany cheered. Everyone loved the idea.

As the friends started gathering snow, they noticed Ona the Eagle soaring toward them. She landed on a rock and said, "Hello, Friends! I just came from visiting with your Grandpaw, Bethany.

I'm so sorry that he has been sick. I brought some of your favorite hot chocolate to brighten your day." Bethany nodded and thanked her. As Ona glided away, she announced,

"I will drop this off at your cave."

"Let's create a great big bear as our snow animal," Riley suggested. The crew collected branches, rocks, and pinecones. They worked together to build the largest snow bear they had ever seen.

The friends looked up proudly at their snow bear.

He was magnificent!

After they finished playing, Bethany invited her friends back to her cave to enjoy Ona's delicious gift. They sipped their warm drinks and talked about the best parts of the day. Feeling grateful, Bethany voiced, "I loved making the snow bear. He reminds me of my Grandpaw." But then she looked sad. Suddenly, Bethany felt so many emotions all jumbled up at once.

Martin patted her paw. "Building the snow bear was my favorite part, too," he agreed. Bethany spoke about Grandpaw...her worries about him being sick, and how she was missing their special adventures. The friends joined in with many of their own stories of love and laughter with Grandpaw. With full bellies and hearts, they said goodnight and headed home to their beds.

The next day, the friends went back to Bethany's cave.
But something was wrong. She was not there. Faye shouted,
"Wait, I have an idea!" as she took off into the forest.
They found Bethany next to the snow bear, quietly crying.

She whispered, "My Grandpaw died.
It happened early this morning. I miss him."

The crew felt sad. No one knew what to say at first, so they sat with her in silence. Bethany's heart was heavy, but she felt comforted having her friends by her side. After a few minutes, Riley said, "Grandpaw will always be remembered. He helped all of the animals in Friendship Grove. He made others want to be brave and kind like him.

We will all miss him."

"Will it always hurt this much?" Bethany asked her friends.
She knew Faye and Martin had grandparents who died too.
Faye didn't talk about losing her grandmother much, but today she shared, "Snowy days are when I miss Nana the most. Together, we used to watch the snow fall. When I feel sad, I close my eyes and feel her warm snuggle. It helps me feel better when I think of her smile and all of the memories we made."

Martin said, "I still miss my Grandma, too, but it's gotten easier over time. We loved to paint together and create our own special recipes to share with our forest friends. Grandma always taught me to remember my strengths. We used to say:

'I am strong. I am creative. I am kind. I can make a difference.' I still say this every day!"

Bethany thought for a moment, then said, "My Grandpaw taught me that we can add happiness to the world with a helpful paw, a smile, a song . . ."

"You sure follow in Grandpaw's paw prints," Riley pointed out.
Bethany grinned and replied, "I do love spreading kindness
and joy to others, just like Grandpaw." The friends paused and
remembered their loved ones. Bethany asked the crew for a hug,
and they all embraced.

Feeling encouraged, Bethany smiled and said, "We loved to whistle through the woodlands, making music together. Grandpaw used to say, 'Look at our pawprints. We're leaving our own special marks along the way!'" Bethany giggled at this memory. Her heart still ached, but she also felt peaceful because she knew Grandpaw would always be a part of her.

His love was still there . . .

And it never left!

Tiny snowflakes danced above them as the crew all looked up into the sparkling night sky. Paw-in-paw, they began to head home.

STOMP, CRACK, BOOM, WHOOSH!

As they marched, their movements sounded like music. Remembering Grandpaw, The Woodland Crew began to whistle. Their beautiful song echoed throughout the fields of Friendship Grove.

Bethany the Bear glanced back and a smile spread over her face as she saw the new pawprints they were making in the snow.

## Discussion Questions:

1. Who experienced the death of a loved one in the book?
2. How did the friends comfort Bethany the Bear and one another?
3. How are The Woodland Crew good friends to each other?
4. What are some happy memories Bethany and the friends have—about their loved ones who have died?
5. How did Bethany and The Woodland Crew celebrate Grandpaw and follow in his paw prints/share kindness with others?

## Questions for Young Readers:

1. Has someone close to you died? How did or does that make you feel?
2. Who or what has helped you manage the pain of loss? (What helps to make you feel better?)
3. How can you be a friend to someone whose loved one has died?
4. What are some happy memories you have with your loved one?
5. What is something about your loved one that you could continue to celebrate?
   It could be a special tradition or a unique character trait they had that you could share with others.

# Suggested Activities that Offer Hope and Encouragement:

1.  Share your favorite stories or memories about your loved one.
2.  Create a memory book, box, or collage with photographs of your loved one.
3.  Write a letter to your loved one in a journal, or place it in your memory book, box, or collage.
4.  Plant a tree to honor your loved one's memory.
5.  Begin an annual tradition to honor your loved one—like making their favorite cake on their birthday or their favorite holiday dish.
6.  Make a craft or draw pictures of your loved one.
7.  Participate in something that was meaningful to your loved one. For example, you can visit a place they loved, listen to their favorite music, or support a cause that was special to them.
8.  Talk to a counselor about how you're feeling. You can also talk to a trusted family member or friend.
9.  If you're religious or spiritual, go to church or engage in prayer.
10. Take a walk in nature, and practice being in the moment with your thoughts and feelings.

# Tools and Tips
## for Parents & Adult Caregivers on Discussing Grief and Loss

- Use simple and direct language. Young children under the age of eight don't need a lot of detailed information. Kids' attention spans at this age are short, so brief conversations are best.

- Answer questions honestly—but don't offer a lot of additional information. Meet kids 'where they're at'—both emotionally and developmentally.

- Be prepared to come back to the discussion at another time. Although attention is limited and children can only process a little at a time, they may have more questions or comments as they continue to develop. When they are ready to revisit the loss, they might ask questions leading to more detailed information. Again, only answer the question(s) that they ask—which will provide a good indication of what they can process at the time.

- You can encourage children to express their grief by setting an example yourself. By sharing some of your own sadness and anger, you can help them understand their own grief and know that it's okay to share their feelings openly.

- For those who are religious or spiritual, talks of Heaven and reuniting someday can be helpful.

- Discuss what you loved about that person and what impact they made on the world. What special character traits did they have, or traditions that you can carry on individually and as a family?

# About the Author

Lauren Sugalski Mosback is a Licensed
Professional Counselor and Licensed Behavior
Specialist. In her counseling practice and her
children's books, she strives to empower children—by giving them the tools
for navigating challenging situations, coping with their emotions, exploring
their unique strengths, and building self-esteem.

When Lauren was in college, she interned at a Navajo school in New
Mexico, teaching and also working in the school counseling office.
Lauren created the character, Ona, in honor of her time there. This
experience inspired her to pursue a path in the counseling field.

Lauren lives outside of Philadelphia with her husband, four children,
and pup. She loves exploring the outdoors and adventuring with
her family. She finds inspiration from these adventures and
continually strives to learn, grow, and write.

CPSIA information can be obtained
at www.ICGtesting.com
Printed in the USA
BVHW012148071222
653743BV00009B/177